One Moon,

by Laura Godwin

Atheneum Books for Young Readers

Two Cats

illustrated by Yoko Tanaka

New York   London   Toronto   Sydney

One moon.

Two cats
are not asleep.

Cats yawn,

cats stretch,

cats look,

cats LEAP!

One cat watches vans and trucks.

One cat slinks by pigs and ducks.

Paw by paw . . .

cats walk the rails.

Cats comb whiskers,

cats twitch tails.

Cats' eyes gleam,

cats blink twice,

cats get ready,

cats smell . . .

...mice!

Mice zig,

cats zag,

mice run,

cats race,

 mice slink,

cats creep,

mice climb,

cats chase.

Mice hide, cats seek.

Mice dart, cats dash.

Mice edge, cats inch.

Mice crouch, cats . . .

CRASH!

BOOM!

FLASH!

It starts to rain.

Cats and

mice run . . .

... home again.

Two cats look,

then lightly leap.

One sun.

Two cats are
fast asleep.

For Marisa
—L. G.

For Panini, Turi, and Zinfandel . . . and all the other cats in the world!
—Y. T.

ATHENEUM BOOKS FOR YOUNG READERS • An imprint of Simon & Schuster Children's Publishing Division • 1230 Avenue of the Americas, New York, New York 10020 • Text copyright © 2011 by Laura Godwin • Illustrations copyright © 2011 by Yoko Tanaka • All rights reserved, including the right of reproduction in whole or in part in any form. • ATHENEUM BOOKS FOR YOUNG READERS is a registered trademark of Simon & Schuster, Inc. • For information about special discounts for bulk purchases, please contact Simon & Schuster Special Sales at 1-866-506-1949 or business@simonandschuster.com. • The Simon & Schuster Speakers Bureau can bring authors to your live event. For more information or to book an event, contact the Simon & Schuster Speakers Bureau at 1-866-248-3049 or visit our website at www.simonspeakers.com. • Book design by Ann Bobco • The text for this book is set in Bookman Old Style • The illustrations for this book are rendered in acrylic paint on 100% cotton illustration boards. • Manufactured in China • 0611 SCP • First Edition • 10 9 8 7 6 5 4 3 2 1 • Library of Congress Cataloging-in-Publication Data • Godwin, Laura. • One moon, two cats / Laura Godwin ; illustrated by Yoko Tanaka. — 1st ed. • p. cm. • Summary: Two cats, one in the city and one in the country, chase mice before going to sleep. • ISBN 978-1-4424-1202-6 (hardcover) • ISBN 978-1-4424-3491-2 (eBook) • [1. Stories in rhyme. 2. Cats—Fiction. 3. City and town life—Fiction. 4. Country life—Fiction.] I. Tanaka, Yoko, ill. II. Title. • PZ8.3.G5465On 2011 • [E]—dc22 • 2009053697